$\mathcal{I}$t's only the wind.
     She is busy sweeping
away fall to make room for
winter. Time for sleep now.

It's Only the Wind

Written and Illustrated by
Mindy Dwyer

WESTWINDS
PRESS®

For Kenji, and Toshi, and all the kids in Bear Valley who listened to the wind . . . Jack, Katey, Sean, Katie, Molly, Rosie, Martin, Cameron, Mariah, Andrea, Clark, Bridget, and Heidi.

Text and illustrations © 2017 by Mindy Dwyer

Library of Congress Cataloging-in-Publication Data

Names: Dwyer, Mindy, 1957- author.
Title: It's only the wind / by Mindy Dwyer.
Other titles: It is only the wind
Description: Portland, Oregon : WestWinds Press, [2017] | Summary: At bedtime, a
    child asks his mother questions about the wind, the noise it makes, and why it
    blows. Includes page of facts about wind.
Identifiers: LCCN 2016054689 (print) | LCCN 2017032222 (ebook) |
    ISBN 9781513260754 (ebook) | ISBN 9781513260747 (hardcover)
Subjects: | CYAC: Winds—Fiction. | Bedtime—Fiction. | Mother and child—Fiction.
Classification: LCC PZ7.D9635 (ebook) | LCC PZ7.D9635 It 2017 (print) | DDC [E—dc23
LC record available at https://lccn.loc.gov/2016054689

Printed in China

Edited by Michelle McCann
Designed by Vicki Knapton

Published by WestWinds Press®
An imprint of

GRAPHIC ARTS
BOOKS®

GraphicArtsBooks.com

room broom

sweep sleep

Mama!
Why does the
wind blow?

She has lots to do.
She sails the seeds away
to their new homes to wake
up one spring day.

Close your eyes, sweetie pies.

blow home

away day

The wind is loud!
How can we
sleep?

Sometimes the wind runs wild.
She kicks up the soil and
sends it down to the valley below.

Now it's time to go to bed.

go below

Mama!
The wind is pounding!

She's just working hard,
rolling big waves onto rocks
to make sand for the beaches.

Night-night, little ones.

rocking

rolling

reach

beach

Do you hear
a whistle?

That's a Chinook wind sliding down the mountain eating up all the snow. Tomorrow will be bright and warm.

Sweet dreams!

warm wind

Is the
wind laughing?

Yes, she's a playful breeze
where birds glide and kites fly.
Settle down, please.

It's only the wind.

flies

glides

Mama!
The wind is howling.
Is she sad?

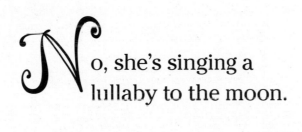
No, she's singing a
lullaby to the moon.

You'll be asleep soon.

Singing Soon

howling moon

Listen . . . it's quiet.
Where did she go?

Back to the sky, where
the wind blows hard or
sometimes soft or not at all.

Hush . . . it's only the wind.

Wind Is a Wonder! It has no shape, smell, or taste of its own—it is invisible! Wind can be powerful enough to knock down trees or gentle enough to sneak up and tickle the back of your neck.

Wind Is Moving Air. Hot air is lighter so it rises up high, and cold air is heavier so it sinks down low. When there is a difference in temperature, wind tries to keep things in balance, so it blows from high to low. The greater the temperature difference, the stronger the wind.

Wind Helps Plants Grow. Many plants depend on wind to spread their seeds. It's the most important pollinator, even more than bees.

Wind Makes Weather. Wind spreads the sun's heat around the world, giving our planet a more moderate climate. Without wind, most places would be too hot or too cold to grow food. Wind also blows moisture that rises into the air above oceans and onto the land to make rain, ice, or snow.

Wind Causes Erosion. Wind can change the landscape as it sweeps sand, dust, and dirt across the land. When wind deposits dust over a large area, it can create a rich farming soil called loess.

Wind Makes Waves. By blowing across the surface of the ocean, the wind makes waves. Beaches are then pounded by waves, slowly crushing rock into tiny grains of sand.

Winds Have Names. People around the world give the wind different names. The Chinook wind, or "snow eater," blows across the Rocky Mountains, bringing warm, dry air that melts snow and raises winter temperatures dramatically.

Wind Helps Birds. Birds can rest their wings and soar high in the sky by riding pockets of warm air that rise. When moving air runs into a cliff, mountain, or building, that air flows up and over the obstacle. Birds can "ride" these currents, like waves in the sky.